I0728037

Prometheus: An Alien Scifi Romance

DEMELZA CARLTON

ONE

"You guys have no idea how much I need this right now," Prometheus said, sinking into what had to be the most comfortable chair in the Colony.

"To lose all your credits to your closest friends? Any time, brother, any time," Ghost said.

"Now, now. We're not actually gambling here. That would require a licence that Forge doesn't have," Vulcan said, setting the poker set down on the table. "I'm not paying for a gambling licence just because a famous news anchor has a big mouth."

"Besides, we all know the big gambling in the Colony happens at the Arena. Fortunes made and lost every night, or so I hear," Achilles said, settling in the twin to Ghost's chair, which creaked ominously under his weight.

Prometheus raised an eyebrow. "And what's your tip for the next dragon battle? I think it's time the dragon won for once, don't you?"

Achilles grinned. "Ah, tonight, you mean? I won't object to that." He rubbed his hands together.

Vulcan held up his hand. "First, before we break out the chips, I have a favour to ask. Our chef has a new menu I'd like you to try. Honest opinions only, please. Oh, and thanks to Nihal's latest brewing efforts, she's matched brand new beers to the dishes. She would like opinions, too, please."

Ghost held up his tablet. "Video it all and

send it to her. Prometheus, you're the best man with a camera." He tossed the tablet across the table, and Prometheus caught it.

"Right. First, the food," Vulcan said, beckoning a waitress forward. "Prometheus, I've been saving this one until you had time to try it, seeing as you're the connoisseur and all, this being your favourite."

Prometheus didn't have a favourite food, and he opened his mouth to say so.

Too late. The waitress revealed a massive platter of what appeared to be ribs, thickly coated in a sticky sauce that smelled like the devil had stolen it from heaven to damn him.

The others made appropriately appreciative noises, but Prometheus pushed the platter across the table, away from him, before folding his arms across his chest. "I hate to tell you this, but I'd have to be starving to eat those tiny strips of meat full of bone and gristle. Now, if you slathered one of those vat grown fillet steaks in that sauce, or maybe some chicken…"

Vulcan's mouth hung open. "But you love ribs! I distinctly heard you tell Zeus back on the *Truella* that those were your favourite ration packs. There were real tears in your eyes when he ate the last one. I'd swear it on my life!"

Prometheus laughed. "Tears of laughter I fought to hold back, I swear. I hate ribs almost as much as chicken wings. All that work for such tiny bits of meat? You should know I'm far too lazy for that. In all the time you've known me, have you ever seen me eat ribs?"

Vulcan's face fell. "Stars, I can't believe it. I never thought…not that it matters. If I told you there wasn't any meat in them at all, would it change things? They're completely plant based protein, grown on 3D printed bone. The sauce isn't quite so virtuous, though. Duck fat, mixed with honey and one of Nihal's special bourbon spirits, as well as my chef's secret blend of herbs and spices. I thought if you enjoyed them, we could add them to our menu. But now…"

Achilles pulled the platter to his side of the table. "I'll eat them. Get the big baby his steak in sauce." The sound of cracking bones echoed ominously through the empty function room. Achilles could be such an animal sometimes.

More food arrived, including Prometheus's steak, and conversation died until the plates were empty. Compliments went to the chef, with the only complaint being a desire for larger portions, before Vulcan finally consented to break out the poker set he'd liberated from the *Titanic*, to take on the *Truella*.

The talk turned to work, the one thing Prometheus didn't want to talk about. He listened to Vulcan's description of Forge's upcoming entertainment and new liquor business, Achilles' plans for new spectacles in the Arena, before Ghost told them a terrifying tale about his last death-defying rescue.

"What about you, Mr News Anchor? Are you the richest man in the Colony yet, or just the most famous?" Vulcan asked.

He was pretty sure Vulcan was the most famous, especially after his performance at the Thanksgiving Festival, but Prometheus forced himself to smile. "Actually, I might not be a news anchor for much longer. Arnold, my boss, thinks what the news needs is a more feminine, caring face than mine. My ratings have been steadily going down since the war ended, and except for a few news stories – most of them involving our resident superhero, Ghost, here – it's pretty much been a year long slide into obscurity for me."

Cries of disbelief came from everyone at the table.

"Who in the stars do they think could tell the news better than you?" Vulcan asked.

Prometheus grimaced. "Koharu, the morning show host."

"Who?"

Being replaced by someone no one had heard of sank his ego even worse. "She's one of the hosts on the morning show. She spends half her time gasping at everything the infomercial guests say during their sales pitch, and the other half reporting useless news items like a hundred ways to turn a ration bar into a gourmet meal or six ways to make a coverall look sexy."

"The only way to make a coverall sexy is to take it off, and do it well," Vulcan said.

They all nodded in agreement.

"As for the ration bar thing…"

They all sat in silence, contemplating the completely unappetising, chewy protein and nutrients that constituted a ration bar.

Vulcan just shook his head. "When Forge first opened, we tried to use the ration bars in some of the food, but we tossed it all in the recycler. The only way to make a gourmet meal with a ration bar is to use the ration bar as a plate, or a rolling pin."

"Or a meat tenderiser."

Prometheus just shook his head. "It doesn't matter what news stories she tells, or even what I report on. There's nothing I can do to increase the ratings, because there's no real news. And if there's no actual news, no one's going to be watching, glued to their screens. The war's over, and so's my career. I guess I should go back to what I did before. Maybe the new cabaret club is hiring."

Achilles looked thoughtful. "Now, don't do anything crazy. You need to do what I do when numbers are down. Give your audience something big."

"Even I'm not a big enough arsehole to want the war back. I like peace as much as anyone."

"Well, what news stories have performed best for you since we arrived at the Colony?"

Prometheus thought for a moment. "The rescue ones. Whenever Ghost saves someone. That time someone got lost under the ice on Gaia. Stories where there's high stakes, and a bit of adventure."

Vulcan frowned. "What was the thing on Gaia?"

"Oh, someone got sucked under the ice, and one of the other team members was so disturbed by what he saw, he gave an interview about how aliens had abducted her. He even described their tentacles, curling around her as they dragged her under. It was a few weeks ago, around Valentine's Day…"

Vulcan nodded. "Ah, yeah, I was busy then. It was my first Valentine's Day with Hestia, and I had big plans."

"Must have missed that one, too. That's when I proposed to Maia," Ghost said.

Achilles shrugged. "Don't expect me to remember. I only pay attention to monsters in the Arena. If they'd caught an alien, though…now that would be a battle to see." He looked misty eyed for a moment, before he cleared his throat and became serious again. "Any other stories that got a lot of viewers?"

"Not that I can think of. Oh, wait. There have been a few pranks that got a lot of views. That time someone poured a heap of detergent into one of the Metropolis fountains, burying the square in bubbles. People were sliding around it like they were ice skating."

"So, good news stories, jokes, and high stakes. Something's bound to happen that'll tick at least two of those boxes. And if it doesn't, just do what I do – fake it." Achilles nodded.

Prometheus stared at him in horror. "I can't fake the news – the whole point about it being news is that it actually happened. There's journalistic integrity, people's right to know the truth, an unbiased voice in a world of advertising and political messages…if I make it up, it's not news, it's propaganda!" He'd quit his job and spend the rest of his life scrubbing toilets rather than pump out propaganda. He had to draw the line somewhere.

"What about April Fool's Day?" Ghost piped up. "I mean, traditionally, all the news outlets run fake news stories then. Not propaganda, but stories that are just close enough to the truth to be believable, while being complete nonsense in reality. Something funny, but that won't actually hurt anyone."

"Maybe…" Prometheus began, the whisper

of an idea swirling through his mind.

"What are you thinking?" Vulcan asked eagerly.

Prometheus shook his head. "I'm not sure yet. I'd need to think about it a bit longer, and I might need some help…maybe some expert advice to make it sound believable…"

"We're in," the other three said in unison.

For the first time in days, Prometheus grinned. "Oh, this is going to be good."

TWO

Some days, Pandora wished she'd gone into early childhood education. Fighting toddlers would be a cakewalk compared to her current job.

"But I need it!"

"It's mine!"

"I had it first!"

Then again, three grown men arguing over a piece of lab equipment wasn't that different to toddlers with a favourite toy.

Pandora took a deep breath. "The chromatograph is booked in hourly blocks. You can book in advance, or, if no one is using it, you can book the current hour for yourself. However, if it's in use, then you need to book a block of time in the future, or wait until whoever is using it is done. According to the current schedule…" She swiped her tablet, pulling up the schedule, then squinted at it. "Ah, I believe Magneto has booked it for this afternoon."

"Yesssss!" Magz pumped his fist in the air.

"But you weren't using it!" Rusty whined.

"My samples took longer to prepare than I expected. Feral was hogging all the titanium crucibles and I had to wait until the wash cycle was finished!" Magz protested.

Feral held up his hands. "Hey, don't go blaming me. I'd have had my samples done yesterday if you hadn't left all the washing up in the sink last night. It's your fault I had to do them today. If you'd cleaned up after yourself, I'd have had all mine done and dusted yesterday!"

"No one was using it, so I automatically assumed no one needed it, and I do, so…"

"But I need it!"

Pandora summoned a professional smile, one she hoped didn't look too like a grimace. "The chromatograph is booked to Magneto for the whole afternoon. I suggest the rest of you discuss with him whether it'll be available again today, or whether you'll need to book your own slots some time in the future."

"You can't do that!"

"Now look here, you – "

Never had Plato's voice over the intercom been more welcome. "Dora, delivery for you!"

Pandora turned on her heel and headed for Reception, ignoring the shouts of the three infantile geologists behind her to their pissing contest.

But Reception was empty.

Had Plato summoned her for a fake delivery to save her from those idiots? She hadn't thought he had it in him. She had to thank him.

She rapped smartly on his office door. "Plato? It's me, Pandora," she said.

The door remained closed. "I had them put the delivery in your office. See that you deal with it before the execs arrive this week."

Of course, when the big bosses would arrive was anyone's guess. If they turned up at all. But Pandora knew if she didn't deal with the delivery, they'd arrive within the hour, and she'd never hear the end of it.

So, "Sure thing," she said, heading for her office. Well, what had been her office until someone had mistaken it for a store room and filled it to the ceiling with sample crates. Did Plato even know how big the delivery was?

She suspected if he did know, he hadn't cared.

Swearing softly, she scanned the label on the nearest crate, bringing up its chain of custody record in the database. Originally taken on Gamma just before the war started, only recently discovered in the hold of a scout vessel turned warship when it was purchased by Vasse Prospecting to be refitted for survey work – the *Truella*. A better name for a survey vessel than a warship, in Pandora's opinion. She hoped the higher ups at Vasse didn't change the name.

Speaking of names…there sure seemed to have been a lot of them on this particular survey team, all taking samples that got left behind. Prometheus, Vulcan, Achilles, Ghost…she didn't recognise any of them, which was odd. After a year of managing Vasse's labs on the Colony, she'd met pretty much every active geology team in the Altan System. Perhaps they worked for some rival mining company she hadn't heard of. A company Vasse had likely bought out, if the samples were here. Usually the geology team handled processing of their own samples, but if the team who'd taken these samples wasn't here, they'd be sitting in the crates for a bit longer until the team turned up.

Unless they hadn't survived the war. That

would explain why the samples had been forgotten. In the absence of the original survey team, she'd have to ask Plato who to give the samples to.

Wincing, she headed back to Plato's office. She hated to do it, but she knocked again.

"What is it?" Plato growled through the closed door.

"Uh…it's me again. The delivery is rock samples from Gamma. Can you remind me who's prospecting on Gamma, so I can give them the samples?"

Plato coughed out a laugh. "No one's prospecting on Gamma, silly girl. It's far too hot for a survey team. The EV suits would melt in minutes."

Pandora's heart sank. Was that what had happened to the survey team? They'd died on the planet's surface, roasted alive? She shuddered. What a horrible way to go.

But if the survey team was dead… "Who should I give them to, then?"

"Whoever has time to spare. There's always

one or two in this lazy lot who race through the lab work so they can have a holiday while everyone else is still working, until the ship's ready to head out again. Find out who's free, and make them do it."

Pandora made a face at Plato's closed door. Getting the geologists to do anything they didn't want to do was an exercise in futility, but if Plato himself couldn't be arsed, then she'd have to at least try.

Maybe today would be her lucky day.

There were three people in the break room, seated around an empty biscuit tub.

"Those were supposed to last us all week – I didn't even see the order come in!" Pandora wailed. Usually, it was delivered to her office, but the boxes must have blocked access. Stars take those samples.

Tits held up his half eaten bikkie. "You snooze, you lose," he drawled, taking an exaggeratedly large bite. Judging by the shower of crumbs that landed amid the drift already adorning his lab coat, Tits had eaten most of them. He boasted his name had come from his talent at finding titanium, but even Pandora knew it was because he had bigger breasts than she did, wobbling over a beer gut that should have been an impossibility on ship rations.

Pandora shook her head. The last thing she wanted to think about was Tits's tits. She pasted a bright smile on her face. "Well, it's doubly lucky you're here, then. I've just had a load of pre-war samples arrive, unclaimed samples, so if you have an hour or two spare to test them for me, you can put your name on the claim if there's a bonus for finding a rich vein."

Pally crammed the last of his biscuit into his mouth before he said, "Don't be stupid. That's not how bonuses work. You have to take the samples at the site, do all the testing, put in the bonus claim, and you only get paid after it's been independently tested, and they can actually extract the ore. It all has to be documented, every step of the way. Whoever took the samples has first claim, no matter who does the first round of testing. And if they were taken before the war, anything's bound to have been mined by now."

"The samples are Vasse property, found sealed in their original crates aboard a salvaged ship. I'm sure Vasse will be grateful to whoever does the testing, especially if they turn out to be a rich vein no one's tapped before," Pandora said. "If the original owners were going to lay claim to them, surely they'd have done so by now. They probably died in the war."

Rhodie narrowed his eyes. "Where were the samples taken?"

"Gamma," Pandora said. There. Like Plato said, they couldn't have been mined yet, if EV suits melted on Gamma.

All three men laughed.

"Stardust," Rhodie said. "No one could have survived taking samples on Gamma. No point mining there, either. Find some other dupe to do your testing. I'm not wasting my time. Whatever's on Gamma, it's where no one can get it."

The other two nodded their agreement.

Pandora's heart was hiding somewhere in her left shoe, it had sunk so low. She sighed, and headed out to find someone else to ask.

By day's end, she was heartily sick of the sound of her colleagues' laughter, and she still had an office full of boxes no one else would touch.

Looked like she'd have to do the testing herself. It'd serve them all right if she found a rich source of....something, in one of the samples. She'd blow her first bonus on biscuits, and keep them all to herself.

She set to work.

THREE

"You look like you're plotting to blow up the Colony. Tell me you're not that stupid."

Prometheus looked up to meet Nihal's gaze, noting how her lips pressed angrily together, and wished there was something he could say that would acquit him of stupidity, but it was far too late for that.

"The only bombshells I drop are explosive news stories. I am and always have been a pacifist," he said.

Her brows lowered further. "Yeah, I remember. You went to pieces when war broke out."

And made the biggest mistake of his life – a one night stand with Nihal that he wished had never happened. Their friendship hadn't been the same since.

"Nihal, what happened that night…" he began, not sure how to continue.

"Was the sort of crazy thing two friends do when they heard that the world was ending. The war, the end of the *Titanic*, the kind of grief that swallows you whole…we both needed someone that night, and as we were the only people aboard the *Truella*, that's how it went down. What happened, happened, and it'll never happen again. Don't even think about it, and I never want to talk about it again. Lots of other, more regrettable mistakes happened during the war. Let's just chalk it up as one of them, and…forget it ever happened."

The whole night had been a blur, numbness brought on by the onset of war, and he had very little in the way of clear memories of it. Just the horror of waking up naked beside her, knowing what they'd done, which could never be undone. He wished he could forget that moment.

But he didn't say that. Instead, he bowed his head and said, "As you wish."

"Now, if you're granting wishes, I hope they include a feature on the news about our latest business venture. I think Nihal should do the interview, but we all know she doesn't want to do it, and as I have a higher profile in the Colony, it'll probably have to be me. So, when are we doing this?" Vulcan asked.

As if this conversation couldn't get more awkward. "Actually, I came to ask a favour. To do with that thing we were talking about on poker night."

Vulcan grinned. "Ah, that thing! So you've come to discuss an exchange of favours." Was it Prometheus's imagination, or had Vulcan's smile turned predatory?

Then again, Prometheus owed Vulcan a few

favours, so his calling one in shouldn't be surprising.

"Come into my office," Vulcan continued. "Unless Nihal had more wishes for you first?"

Nihal shook her head. "I'm good, boss. I'll take care of the bar while you talk him out of whatever he's plotting."

There was no point denying it. They might not have been close lately, but she knew him too well for him to lie. In fact, he should hustle to Vulcan's office, before she guessed his whole plan and blurted it out in the bar. That would ruin the joke entirely.

Prometheus didn't dare relax until Vulcan had clicked his office door shut.

"You want to go first?" Vulcan asked.

Prometheus nodded. "I need your help with the video for my April Fool's Day feature. I've gone through all the footage we took on Gamma, and I think there's some filming Achilles did. We were fooling around, not really working at the time, but I think it could be what I need. It'll need some editing, though, which is where you come in. I mean, sure, I can use my editing software to get what I need, but it'll be slow and time consuming, and even then it might look like the video's been altered. But if you use a little of your magic to make the illusion appear real...."

Vulcan folded his arms across his chest. "I'll want a minimum of one interview, to go public in a month or two, when we're ready to launch to the public. Maybe more, depending on how much work your video needs."

"Whatever you need, assuming I still have airtime to offer. We're all going to be drinking something, so it's better it comes from a reputable company with safety standards, instead of jury rigged stills using stewed ration bars to brew random rotgut." Prometheus grimaced. He suspected the recipes had come from Koharu's show, or somewhere equally dubious, because he knew Metropolis Hospital had dealt with an increasing number of poisoning cases, most of which involved methanol and alcohol. "Maybe we should schedule a longer feature, where you or Nihal show the brewing process, so people know how it's done properly. We haven't run any stories on poisonings from the illegal stills, because the Watch don't want to encourage the practice, but if we run a piece on legal brewing, with the products available at a reasonable price…you're not just brewing for Forge, right? We're talking about budget beers for normal people?"

Vulcan nodded. "Of course we'll have a range of products. Budget beers right up to luxury liqueurs, all using locally grown ingredients. Not to mention our range of Forge fizzes, available in take home bottles."

"Sounds good, actually. I can get the basic details from you now, sort a list of rough interview questions for you in the next few days, then schedule the interview and a tour of the production facilities early next week, if you like?"

"That works well. Mondays are usually quiet here, and if we film just before lunch, Nihal should be nice and fresh to show you and your camera crew around. Right, now show me the Gamma footage, and tell me what you need me to do with it." Vulcan rubbed his hands together.

Prometheus pulled up the video on his tablet, then transferred it to the big screen on the wall. It looked a bit grainy, but he'd be able to clean that up. "It was when you dumped a canteen of water over me, to wash off the dust and it sort of went poof...I want some light there, a bit of a glow, to make it look more dramatic."

"How dramatic? Like you're on fire and about to explode, something subtle just to highlight it, or something in between?"

Prometheus watched the video play through once, then restarted it so he could see it a second time. "I'm thinking...like it was streaming lava. I'd use the shots where I took an actual lava bath, but the lens steamed up so much, the footage is useless."

Vulcan raised his eyebrows. "Are you sure?

I'm sure you have a lot of female viewers who'd watch the broadcast over and over just to see you in the bath."

Prometheus spread his hands wide. "I'm just as nude in these shots, remember. We all were. Ghost said protective gear caused more problems than it solved, and we knew the risks. We were fine."

Vulcan was so intent on the video, he didn't seem to be listening. "The light show will look more dramatic if you change the ambient lighting to night time. Even overcast day on Gamma was bright. You'll want contrast. What impression are you trying to give with the lights?"

This was the dancer, the artist, talking, not the business man now. Vulcan was frighteningly good at being both. But he also understood the artistry of a particular camera angle as well as the effect it would have on his target audience.

Prometheus thought for a long moment, then said, "I want something like the Gaia footage, where that probe's sensor array moved just right, so that guy believed it was alive, and had taken his colleague, instead of her just falling in."

"You want alien tentacles."

Prometheus laughed. "Who doesn't? I know for a fact that downloads of tentacle erotica tripled the week we broadcast that story, and it stayed high for weeks. Ask your librarian friend if you don't believe me."

"Sexy alien tentacles, or scary ones?"

"Neither. There's sound in the video, and even if we don't play it, because I'm sure I swore, I'm clearly laughing. I want them to feel what I did. That it was really cool. To just watch…in wonder."

"Wonderful tentacles."

"Yeah. Can you do that?"

Vulcan stared at the video. "I think so, but it'll take some time. For light to dance so well it evokes a sense of wonder, you're asking for art. Real art."

"Well, you're the artist. Not me – I just take

pictures of it, and pretend I understand it. I do appreciate it, though. You know that, right?"

Vulcan nodded. "Sure. But it'll cost you two features, including the guided tour with Nihal."

"It's a deal," Prometheus said. He'd consider selling his soul if it meant keeping his job and staying in the Colony. Not that his soul was worth much, but he'd rather keep his job through a harmless April Fool's Day joke, than giving people dangerous recipes to brew substances that could kill them, like Koharu. After all, everyone needed a laugh now and then.

FOUR

By the time Pandora had finished preparing the first batch of samples, everyone else had gone home. Which meant she had access to any of the analysis equipment she needed. The first few showed high iron quantities, which was promising. Okay, it wasn't lithium or some rare metal, but it was still very useful. Not to mention profitable for whoever found it.

High iron content meant more testing, though, to determine what sort of iron ore she had, and whether extraction was worth it. She'd best get those samples prepped now, while the spectrometer did its thing, because she'd never get access to the thermogravimetric analyser when any of the other geologists were in the lab.

When all the testing was complete, she knew it was well past midnight. If she didn't stop now, she'd still be in the lab when the dawn lights turned Colony night into day, and stars knew she wouldn't make it through a full work day without sleep.

She dumped the sample tubes in the sink, figuring she could deal with them in the morning, then stopped. Better that she hide the used tubes in one of the seldom used fume cabinets, where they wouldn't bother anyone. She could wash them up tomorrow, when she had a moment during the day. After she'd had a chance to check the rest of the results. Tomorrow, not tonight, she chided herself. At least she'd have something to look forward to in her otherwise dreary day.

If all the samples were as promising as the first few, she'd be able to afford Colony-grown chocolate. Maybe not every day, but definitely every week. And all the biscuits she could eat.

That was worth working a week's worth of overtime, she decided, as she exchanged her lab coat for a jacket and headed home to her tiny apartment.

FIVE

"This week, my chef has bacon-wrapped chicken breast for you. Vat grown chicken, and plant protein bacon, for anyone who cares. She swears it's as good as anything she ever made on Tito."

It was poker night again, and Vulcan was still using them all as guinea pigs to test out the new menu items. If it had been anyone else, Prometheus might have been tempted to complain, but the food from Forge's kitchen never disappointed. He only wished he could afford to eat Forge food every night.

"Oh, and Prometheus — that video you wanted. One sec, I'll send it through now." Vulcan pulled out his tablet, swiped at it a few times, then put it away. "There."

An alert beeped on Prometheus's tablet, indicating he had a file waiting for him. He set it to play, and found himself nodding before more than a few seconds had passed. Vulcan had done a masterful job.

"Hey, wasn't that the weird dust you got all over you, when you took those rock samples on Gamma? And I said you needed a bath?" Achilles asked, craning his neck so that he could get a better view over Prometheus's shoulder. "Wow, that dust looks even weirder than I remember."

Which meant Vulcan had managed to edit the footage so well, even the men who were there would swear it matched their memories of that day.

"So what do you think?" Vulcan asked.

"I think that this is one April Fool's Day prank that'll go off without a hitch," Prometheus said.

"You going to tell us what the joke is?" Ghost asked.

Prometheus shook his head. "You'll have to watch the midday breaking news broadcast, same as everyone else. Shall we play some poker?"

"Dinner first," Vulcan said.

Right. Best not get ahead of himself.

But this would work. It had to.

SIX

Pandora blinked at her tablet screen. Magnetite? That couldn't be possible. She'd have to retest every single sample, not to mention prepare entire new batches, because she must have done something wrong last night. There couldn't be magnetite on Gamma, because magnetite meant...

An urgent message beeped, and she answered it automatically. "Hi, this is Pandora, Lab Manager at – "

"You need to come and fix this. My lab's been invaded." Magz sounded so affronted, Pandora wanted to ask if the alien invader had insisted on an anal probe.

She sighed. She might wish for aliens, but it was more likely the invader was Feral, borrowing lab equipment again, as though his own lab didn't have exactly the same things.

"On my way," Pandora said, ending the call.

Her heart sank as she marched into Magneto's laboratory. This was the lab where she'd stashed her washing up. Evidently the fume cabinet wasn't as disused as she'd thought.

"Someone's been using my lab at night when I'm not here," Magz announced. He pointed an accusing finger at the contaminated fume cabinet. "Want to know how I found out? It's because they left the lights on!"

The lab lights relied on motion sensors after hours, so she couldn't have left the lights on.

"Do you need to take fingerprints to find the culprit, or can I turn it off now?" Magz asked.

"Do whatever you need to. I'm sure the security logs will show whoever was here last night," Pandora said.

"Good. It's too bright in here," Magz grumbled, crossing the lab to the fume cabinet. He flicked the light switch, but nothing happened, so he flicked it again, before trying it several more times. "Hey, they broke the switch, too!"

Pandora hadn't touched the light switch last night — she'd just shoved her tub of test tubes into it and closed the door. Yet the same fume cabinet was now glowing, lit from within.

Stars, she must have found something radioactive in those samples. She should have stayed to check the results. Was it too late to take iodine pills? Only one way to find out.

"Do you have a radiation detector in here, Magneto?" she asked.

He shrugged. "I thought all the labs had one. It's an alarm that goes off if it detects higher than normal radiation. Cobie set it off on our first day here – he hit paydirt on a cobalt deposit."

She breathed again. If the samples hadn't set off any alarms, then the fume cabinet was sufficient to contain whatever radiation they emitted. That meant it was most likely alpha particles, probably from uranium or radium. Low risk, as long as it stayed shielded in the fume cabinet.

Pandora nodded slowly. "I'll call Maintenance, and see if they can deal with it. In the meantime, don't touch this fume cabinet, and definitely don't open it. If the radiation alarms go off, I want you to leave the lab immediately."

All colour drained from Magneto's face. "Radiation? Stars, no, I'm not working in a lab with anything radioactive! I haven't gotten my breeding bonus yet, and I'm not missing out on it because of some damaged lab equipment." He swept up an armload of loaded test tube racks. "I'm going to go work in Feral's lab until I get the all clear that this one's safe." He hurried out, throwing his final words over his shoulder: "You'll take care of it and tell me when I can come back, right?" He didn't wait for an answer.

Wonderful. Now it was only a matter of time before a verbal explosion occurred in Feral and Rusty's lab. Then again, there wasn't anything she could do unless she sorted out the mess in this lab. She might as well get to work on that – if she could fix things herself, without a call to Maintenance, the sooner she could get some real work done.

She got suited up, checking to make sure her face shield was properly in place, before cracking the seal on the fume cabinet. Pandora counted to ten, waiting for the radiation alarms to go off. Nothing.

She cautiously slid open the door, holding her breath. The safety protocols for uranium and radium mentioned a radioactive gas that would definitely set the alarms off, but they stayed stubbornly silent.

Maybe the cabinet's light switch was faulty

after all, and she'd been worried about nothing.

Her gaze darted to the tub of dirty test tubes she'd left soaking overnight. She was sure she'd left the tub full of water, but there was no sign of it now. Instead, the tubes, tub and part of the bench inside the cabinet were covered in a sort of golden moss. Glowing golden moss.

Pandora swore. Somehow, the Gamma samples must have gotten contaminated. Like that time someone stuck bioluminescent algae on the shower heads on Io Station and the algae had colonised the whole bathroom before anyone noticed. Anyone who'd showered glowed for a week until they'd found a way to sterilise the stuff.

She'd have to do the same here. After she took a small sample of the moss for analysis. Pandora scraped some of the stuff into a clean sample tube, capped it, and then closed the cabinet. She set the controls for a wash and UV sterilisation, which would take several hours, but it was the most effective way to kill off most things.

Of course, she'd barely stuck her hazmat suit into the laundry chute before she heard shouting from the direction of the iron ore lab next door – loud enough to hear through the walls, though she couldn't quite make out the words. Not that she needed to. Rusty or Feral telling Magz to get back to his own lab, most likely.

Sighing, she headed out to break up the fight.

SEVEN

When Pandora's work day ended, she wanted nothing more than to head home and collapse in her bed for the night, but she still had those Gamma samples to deal with. Not to mention that golden moss, or whatever it was.

The moss was easy to deal with. She put a small sample of it into the DNA sequencer in the little-used biology lab, and left it to do its thing while she grabbed a bite to eat.

In the break room, she found there was no

food except for ration bars, which would have to do for dinner, washed down with some much needed coffee. To take her mind off the bar's bland flavour, she took out her tablet so that she could go through the test results one more time.

Every single sample she'd tested last night had massive amounts of magnetite. Unless there was something wrong with the equipment, and stars knew one of the geologists would have complained loudly long before now if there was.

The problem with magnetite was that it only occurred in the presence of oxygen – produced by living organisms. Tiny, algae-like creatures that had just worked away, generation after generation, for millions of years, terraforming a planet for other, more complex life they'd never live to see. That's how they'd found life on Mars, after all, which had been instrumental in helping to terraform the red planet.

But there couldn't be life on Gamma.

Well, unless the Titans had already started

terraforming Gamma and not told anyone. But that didn't explain the magnetite. For magnetite to have formed in the rock beneath Gamma's surface, there had to have been life on Gamma millions of years ago.

Or, more likely, the Titan bioengineers had created some sort of heat-tolerant microbe that accumulated minerals in useful concentrations to facilitate extraction. She'd heard all sorts of stories about the bioengineers in Eden — they were way more advanced than their Earth counterparts.

The DNA sequencer would tell her what the moss was.

But first, she had more rock samples to process.

She made it through two boxes — double last night's effort — before she gave up, a little after midnight. She detoured via the sequencer to see if it had any results yet, but all she got was a stream of error messages, telling her the sample she'd provided was too small for it to extract any DNA. Growling, Pandora prepared three samples for it, much larger than the first, and stuck them in the sequencer. She'd come back and check the results again in the morning. It wasn't like the moss was going anywhere in the meantime.

EIGHT

The next morning, the sequencer greeted Pandora with more flashing error reports. In all three samples, it hadn't been able to find any DNA. The sequencer had to be broken. There couldn't possibly be any other explanation.

Unless the moss wasn't moss at all, but some sort of mineral that crystallised out of the air, catalysed by something in the dust from Gamma.

Well, there was an easy way to check if the sequencer was working. She plucked out a hair, pushed it into a sample tube, and stuck it in the sequencer. If it dared deny she had DNA, then she'd know it was broken. If not…well, then something else was going on here.

Pandora checked the time on her tablet, then the schedule on the chromatograph. If she was quick, she might manage to get another crate of samples processed before anyone else was scheduled to use it. That would bring her total up to four, and she'd only have two left to process tonight before her office would be her own again.

Even better, she could send all the results off to whoever decided what to mine, and she'd find out whether there was a bonus in it for her, working all this overtime and all. Vasse Prospecting paid well, but it was on salary – overtime was just part of the job, when required. Not for the first time, she wondered why she'd never seen anyone else in the office after hours.

Maybe the only reason she did so much overtime was that she was slower at this than anyone else. There were probably far more capable lab managers and technicians who could replace her if Vasse ever found out…

Pandora gulped. Time for a coffee, and hope that by some miracle, there'd be more biscuits in the break room.

When Magneto entered the break room, she had almost finished her coffee, but she wasn't anywhere near convincing herself that eating a ration bar would be almost as good as a chocolate biscuit. What she wouldn't give for one packet of Tim Tams…

"Is the radiation leak in my lab fixed?" he said.

Pandora blinked. Yesterday morning had been so long ago, she'd forgotten. "Yes, the lab's safe to work in." She'd spent half the night there, after all.

"Then why is my fume cabinet still glowing?" he demanded.

Pandora swore. She must have left the UV

steriliser on all night. Worse, the moss-covered tubes still needed cleaning, even if the moss was dead. "That's my fault. I'll fix that right away," she said, tipping out the dregs of her coffee into the sink. She was better off not eating that ration bar, anyway.

Today, the cabinet door didn't want to open. Maybe some of the dead moss had gotten stuck during the cleaning cycle. She leaned her not inconsiderable weight against the door handle, and it moved the tiniest bit. Millimetre by stubborn millimetre, she managed to get the door open wide enough to see inside the cabinet.

And when she did…

"Stars," she whispered. Every bit of the cabinet's surface was covered in a thick layer of moss, with a small, mossy boulder in the middle marking where the tub of test tubes had been yesterday. Well, they probably still were there, under the moss. All of it glowed brighter than the lights overhead.

"Oh, that is disgusting!" Magz complained,

peering over her shoulder. "Get someone to clean that up. I need that cabinet."

Pandora tried to say that she had tried to clean it yesterday, and this was the result of that automatic clean cycle, but Magz seemed too busy with his work to hear her, let alone respond. She had yet to meet an exploration geologist who cared about anything more than his work, and finding that next big mineral deposit.

Besides, none of the geologists would know how to disinfect a fume cabinet that was resistant to normal cleaning methods. She'd probably need to contract a specialist, and in order to do that, she'd have to ask Plato.

To her surprise, he had the door open today.

"Plato, I have a problem with one of the labs. A fume cabinet needs disinfecting…"

"Then do it, and don't waste my time!" Plato snapped.

Pandora managed a pained smile. "I tried, I set off a full wash cycle and irradiated it with

UV overnight, but…"

"I don't care how you do it, just do it! Exec could be here any day, and we can't have the labs looking anything but immaculate. Find a scrubbing brush and scrape it off yourself, if you have to. Can't you see I'm busy?" He glared at her. "Shut the door on your way out."

Pandora waited until she'd closed the door firmly behind her before she blew out a frustrated breath. Physically scrubbing surfaces in a lab only led to more imperfections where contaminants might hide, which required more cleaning, and more cleaning, until you had to replace the equipment altogether. Plato must be really worried about this inspection, if he'd forgotten that.

Then she realised she'd forgotten to tell him about the possibly dodgy DNA sequencer. Replacing that would be more expensive than cleaning a cabinet. She should probably check on that, too.

The sequencer surprised her with a detailed report on her hair's DNA. It might not be able to sequence the moss, but it could identify her, no worries.

What was it, then, if it wasn't moss?

NINE

"Wait, I have a breaking story that has to be the lead on today's show," Prometheus said, breezing past the makeup artist to plant himself firmly in front of Arnold. "I'm late because I only just got the final details now."

Arnold eyed him suspiciously. "A story bigger than the upcoming dragon battle in the Arena?"

Bloody Achilles and his epic battles. "Way bigger than that. Dragons take second place to this." He'd say it to Achilles' face, too, if he was here. Just to see his reaction.

"But the Arena's sponsoring the show! They paid for a heap of advertising..." Arnold began.

"Doesn't matter. We'll still run the ads and all the usual sponsorship stuff. Trust me, the ads will get way more eyeballs with this story than some tired old dragon."

Arnold wagged a finger. "If you're wrong, I'll give Koharu your spot on the evening news, starting tonight."

Inwardly, Prometheus gulped. This was a supernova-sized gamble, and if he lost...well, at least he could say he'd gone out fighting with everything he had. "Not a chance," he said blithely, hoping he sounded more confident than he felt. It didn't help that he'd come last in the most recent poker tournament.

He'd given Vulcan's doctored video to the production team, ready to play it as soon as he'd finished the intro, and they knew him well enough to do as he asked.

Prometheus kept up his usual small talk through hair and makeup, all the way through to light and sound testing in the studio before the camera crew started counting down until the broadcast went live.

Five…

Four…

Three…

Two…

One…

"Good morning, Colony. This is Prometheus with a breaking news story at noon. Alien life has been discovered on Gamma. I repeat, alien life has been discovered by a geological survey team on Gamma…"

TEN

Pandora burst into the break room, where everyone had clustered for lunch in front of the wall screen to watch the news.

"It's aliens!" she burst out. "There's alien life on Gamma!"

Several of them hushed her, while someone dialled up the volume on the wall screen.

How could they not care?

"Don't you understand? For the first time ever, we've discovered an alien species outside our Solar System! This is it! First contact!" she persisted.

Plato turned around to send her a withering glance. "We already know."

But…how? She'd only just worked it out herself. That the samples grew and multiplied in the presence of water like Earth microorganisms, but they didn't have DNA to sequence because they hadn't originated in the Solar System. These Altan aliens had evolved in a completely different environment to anything they'd ever seen before, and even with her background in Martian microbes, she hadn't seen the truth until…

"Geological survey crews, taking samples to evaluate possible mining resources on Gamma, first encountered the alien creatures on a routine survey mission, but their reaction to this phenomenal first contact was nothing less than amazement and awe," the newsreader said.

The newsfeed crossed to a grainy video, tagged at the bottom with a bunch of numbers and the name ACHILLES.

Pandora blinked. She'd seen that name on the sample boxes.

A human figure appeared on the screen. "Are you seeing this? It's…stars, it's amazing. Like nothing I've ever seen before. Are you getting this? It's like it's alive…" Glowing streams of something flowed over the man's body, embracing him like a long-lost brother.

The screen cut back to the news anchor in the studio. "If you're just joining us, this is Prometheus with a breaking news story. Alien life has been discovered on Gamma."

Prometheus. His name was on the boxes, too. In fact, the very samples that had been in those test tubes she'd stashed in the fume cupboard.

"I need to go make a call," she managed to say before she bolted from the break room.

No one even noticed she'd gone.

ELEVEN

They cut to an ad break, and Prometheus seized his glass of water, downing the contents in two big gulps.

Arnold was grinning from ear to ear. "The message boards and forums are exploding with comments, the switchboard can't keep up with the calls, and I estimate half the people in the Colony are tuned into the noon news live! You are a star, Prometheus!"

One of the production assistants came

bustling up. "Mr Prometheus, you need to take this call. It's about the aliens." She held out her tablet for him to take.

Prometheus looked down at the screen. The call was sound only. "Uh, hello?" he said.

"Mr Prometheus?"

"Just Prometheus will do."

"All right. My name is Dr Pandora Box, the laboratory manager at Vasse Prospecting's laboratory facilities here in Metropolis City. I've just recently acquired the rock samples you took on Gamma, not knowing they were actually biological specimens, too, and I'd like to ask…"

Prometheus blinked. Had one of the other guys set this up? Some expert he could interview about his imaginary alien species? It had to be Vulcan.

"Dr Box, would you be willing to appear on the news and do a video interview with me?" he asked.

If Vulcan had arranged this, then of course she would.

"Um…um, yes? I guess?" she said.

Prometheus's gut twinged. Had switchboard made a mistake and sent him a call from a nutter conspiracy theorist instead? If they had…

He swallowed. If they had, then he'd just have to come clean about the whole thing being an April Fool's Day joke earlier than he'd planned, preferably while the woman was live on the news, so they could capture her reaction.

"Dr Box, the commercial break's about to end, so if you're ready, we'll put your video feed onscreen and we can start the interview momentarily," he said.

"Pandora. Please, call me Pandora."

She sounded exactly like an academic who'd never been on the news before. Just the right combination of nerves and bravado. Vulcan had definitely planned this, and he had no idea how he'd manage to thank the man.

"Okay, Doctor Pandora, we'll be going live in thirty seconds. You'll hear me do the intro, then I'll introduce you and greet you, and all you'll have to do is pretend you're just answering the call now, instead of a few minutes ago, and we'll go from there. Ready?"

"Um…yes?"

Prometheus handed the tablet to the production assistant, then grinned toothily at the camera.

Five, four, three, two, one…

"Welcome back to the noon news. If you're just joining us, life has been discovered on Gamma. I have here leading xenobiology expert Dr Pandora Box, PhD, to discuss her findings in more detail…"

TWELVE

Pandora's heart was beating so fast, she couldn't believe it didn't jump right out of her chest and take flight. Though she fumbled it twice, on the third try, she managed to set her tablet up in its stand, pointed at where she sat at her desk, before turning the camera on for the call. Two of the boxes were in view behind her, but so was the label with Prometheus's name on it, so she left them as they were. Props, wasn't that what you called things you wanted in the shot?

She'd had media training years ago, back when an asteroid had struck the station she'd worked on and they'd lost some of their personnel in the resulting decompression, but this was the first time she'd ever put it to use.

"Dr Pandora, are you there?"

Pandora swallowed. "Yes, yes, I'm here. It's a pleasure to talk to you."

On her tablet screen, Prometheus smiled pure sex back. "Oh, I promise, the pleasure is all mine, Doctor. It's not every day I get to speak to an expert on aliens, particularly as this is our first contact with a truly alien species. Can you tell me a bit about our new neighbours?"

As if her and Prometheus would ever live close enough together to share neighbours. He was so far out of his league, he might have been living on Gamma.

"Well, I imagine you know about as much as I do, seeing as you were actually there for first contact. I was lucky enough to receive the rock samples you took on Gamma. Imagine my surprise when I realised I didn't just have a piece of iron ore, but a real, live alien species in my laboratory! At first, they reminded me of some sort of moss or algae, especially with that glow, but when I tried to sequence their DNA…

He asked, she answered, and on the dance went, as if she'd known the steps all her life.

By the end, all she could see was his warm, inviting smile. All she could hear was his rich, velvety voice, coaxing answers out of her that she'd barely even thought about, but now could string together in coherent sentences that even sounded like she knew all about the aliens she'd only identified that morning.

"Thank you, Doctor Pandora, for that illuminating interview. I can't wait to speak to you again about our new alien friends."

She mumbled a response before the screen went dark.

Only then did she dare to breathe…and admit to herself she couldn't wait to hear

Prometheus's voice again. She'd seen him on the news before, of course, but this had been so much more personal. Stars, if he'd asked her to take her clothes off, she would have seriously considered it. No, she'd have done it, without even pausing to think…

"DORA! Get your arse in my office right now!"

Pandora jumped out of her seat and scurried to Plato's office before he could shout again.

"You wanted me, sir?" she asked.

"Do you know what it says on the sign outside the door?" he demanded.

She didn't bother to check. "Uh, your name and job title, sir?" It was a reasonable guess.

He glowered. "No, I mean outside the main door. The sign you can see from the street."

She relaxed. "Oh. You mean Vasse Prospecting Laboratories, unless something's happened to the sign again."

"And who do you work for?"

She suspected he wanted her to say she worked for him, but she knew what her contract said. "Vasse Prospecting Laboratories."

"So did it occur to you, when you were selling Vasse Prospecting's secrets to the press, that they were your secrets to sell?"

Pandora's mouth dropped open. She hadn't sold anything, nor been offered a single credit for her time on the news.

"Of course you didn't think, silly girl. You should have come to me first, and told me about your findings. Then I could have advised you on what to do with this information. The Vasse executives would have needed to approve any release of information to the press, after several articles in peer-reviewed publications, which I would have cast an eye over for you, of course."

As if Plato knew anything about xenobiology, or biology at all. Why, he probably hadn't seen his own dick past his beer gut in at least a decade. No wonder he had an office job – he wouldn't be able to squeeze that belly into an EV suit. Not that she could talk, seeing as most standard issue EV suits were made for men who had no hips or butt to speak of, and her generous curves were a tight fit when she'd had to don an EV suit, but…

Pandora shook her head. Her thoughts were wandering, and they shouldn't be.

"Thank you, sir, but…"

Her tablet, which she'd somehow grabbed on her way out of her office, chimed an incoming call alert. Without thinking, she answered the call.

"Dr Pandora?"

It was him! She wanted to melt into a puddle on the floor at the sound of his voice.

"Yes?"

"I can't thank you enough for what I believe is the best interview I've ever been honoured to be a part of. In fact, I'd like to start by taking you out to dinner on Saturday, when I give you my solemn promise that I will make sure you have the best night of your life."

She needed new underwear. Or no underwear. Or…

"Sure," she managed to say.

"See you Saturday at six, then? I'll pick you up," he said.

She nodded, then ended the call before she could embarrass herself further.

"So that man-whore seduced it out of you. I suppose that's to be expected," Plato said. "I can't imagine he'd sleep with you for any other reason. He'll dump you when he's done with you, just so you're warned, and you won't get any time off if you're silly enough to break your heart over him. He's only boning you to get the story."

Pandora drew herself up. "I haven't – "

"Oh, don't bother. When I tell the executives it was love that motivated you, not money, they might actually let you keep your job. It's better than selling out, I suppose. Anyway, you're to focus on this alien thing for the foreseeable future. Everything you can find out about it. Orders from the top. But I expect you tell me first, not him. No matter how hard he pumps you for information." Plato grinned, then frowned. "No, I don't even want to think about you having sex. I just ate, after all. Go, get back to work, so I don't have to look at you." He made shooing motions.

Pandora was only too happy to escape.

THIRTEEN

"That was brilliant. How did you even hear about it? Aliens. Real aliens," Arnold marvelled, taking a long swig from his beer. One of the samples from Forge's new brewery, Prometheus noted.

Prometheus shrugged. "You know me. I hear a lot of things no one else does. I knew someone who knew someone, plus there's the added bonus that I was on the initial survey team. I still had the old survey footage, so I dug it out, cleaned it up, and…well." He shrugged, doing his best to look modest. He wasn't sure it would have fooled anyone who truly knew him, but he'd only been working with Arnold for a year. Arnold hadn't even realised the story was supposed to be a joke. Well, until Pandora had called. Then it had become deadly serious, all humour forgotten.

"Well, I think it's your best story yet. We've been showing short clips all week, building buzz for the next report. Does your doctor have any more to tell you about the aliens?"

"Ah…" He hadn't spoken to her since April Fool's Day, when he'd given in to the crazy urge to ask her out. Thankfully, she'd accepted, and he was really looking forward to tomorrow night. "I'm sure I'll be the first to hear when she does," Prometheus lied. He'd have to ask her about her work tomorrow.

"Make sure to get an update before tomorrow night. I've scored us an exclusive interview with Vasse CEO, Stella Vasse, and I want you to ask her all the hard questions. See what they're doing to study and save the aliens, or save us from them, if that's what we need."

Prometheus choked on his drink. "I don't work Saturday nights! I can't interview her then!"

Arnold laughed, but it had an edge to it. "What do you mean, you can't? Of course you can. Vasse insisted she'd only do the interview if it was you asking the questions."

"But…I have a date. With Pandora." He didn't like how small his voice sounded.

"Excellent! Bring her along. We can set the expert and the CEO against one another, and watch them explode. It's brilliant. Brilliant! That's why you're my favourite news anchor, Prometheus. Just when I think I've secured the jewel in the crown, you pull out something so blindingly brilliant, it puts everyone else in the shade." He belched, then tossed his beer bottle in the recycler. "See you tomorrow." He left.

Prometheus crumpled in his chair. He'd been looking forward to his date all week. Now, he was dreading telling Pandora he'd somehow tricked her into doing an interview with some battle axe of a CEO who would probably take them both apart piece by piece.

He closed his eyes. No. Dissecting the guests was the interviewer's job. His, not the CEO's. He set down his barely touched beer. No time for alcohol now. He had a planetload of research to do, on Vasse and its owner, plus the charming Pandora.

Tomorrow, that CEO wouldn't know what hit her.

FOURTEEN

Pandora walked into the infested iron ore lab the next morning, only to find it had acquired a new population overnight. Humans, instead of aliens, walking around purposefully in their lab coats like they owned the place.

"Sorry," she said automatically, backing out again.

"Doctor Box! Oh, I'm so glad you're here. We've spent all morning unloading the new equipment and getting set up, but we couldn't find your research plan anywhere." The woman held out her hand. "I'm Aliana, the Head Technician."

"I know," Pandora said, but she shook the woman's hand anyway. "Don't you usually work in the geology labs?"

"Well, yes, but we've been reassigned to your project, which is much more exciting. Aliens! Who'd have thought?" Aliana's smile looked dreamy, before she shook herself. "Sorry, Doctor Box, I'm just so excited to get started. Your research plan?"

Pandora blinked. Yesterday, her only plan had been to work out how to get rid of the strange moss in the fume cabinet. Now... She took a deep breath. "Actually, I'd appreciate your help on that, if that's all right. You're familiar with all the equipment and your staff's expertise, so it makes sense that for a plan to work, I'll need your head as well as mine."

Aliana nodded. "Then we need coffee and doughnuts."

Pandora's mouth watered. She couldn't

remember the last time she'd had doughnuts. Not since she'd left Earth…

"I'll order some, and we can go to the break room to get started while we wait," Aliana said.

Pandora could only nod. She grabbed a notepad and her tablet, then headed for the break room.

Feral was there, munching on what looked like the last biscuit.

Stars, she must have missed another delivery. She needed to buy her own and lock them in her desk.

"So, I heard you've been sleeping with that hotshot reporter, and that's how you got on the news," Feral said. He sniggered. "We're all betting on what you had to do to get him to do it. I mean, it's gotta be anal, or seriously good oral. I said it'd have to be both, and you'd have done ass to mouth because there's no way someone that famous would have…not with you. I mean, if you were even half sexy, half the guys here would've had you already, but…you're…you. So, it's ass to mouth, right?

I win the bet?"

Pandora couldn't even find the words to respond to that. Why in the stars did everyone think she was sleeping with Prometheus?

"I knew it!" Feral shouted, running out of the room. "I win!"

Aliana stepped into the room, giving a delicate shudder. "Oh, I will be so glad when the Sex Doll Crew set sail for some faraway rock. A more archaic bunch of men I never hope to meet."

"What did you call them?"

Aliana giggled. "Why, they're the Sex Doll Crew, of course. They all chipped in and bought a decommissioned sex bot they share when they're out in the black. It has all the holes, but the robotic bits don't work. The whole crew use it, passing it from bunk to bunk. Or maybe it has its own bunk, I'm not sure. They tried to get one of my techs to sanitise it for them once. Ugh, I've seen more sanitary sewer pipes. Disgusting. I reported it to the Watch, and now it has to stay aboard the ship, because it won't pass quarantine. Now the only action they see onplanet is at the brothels, where the staff are wise to them now, and charge them extra."

"How did I not know any of this?"

Aliana shrugged. "Well, you're their superior, aren't you? They're hardly going to talk openly in front of you. Whereas us techs are scum to them, servants to order around, or ignore. Which is why I'm so thrilled to be working with you! So, where do we start?"

Pandora shook her head, hoping to clear it of the images of sex dolls and other assorted depravity. "I'm thinking growth plates, with various different media. We want to know everything. What it likes, what it doesn't. A range of temperatures. Radiation exposure. It likes water and UV, but didn't seem to be doing much of anything in the sample tubes, so we should be looking at a higher temperature range, like the original conditions on Gamma. Chromatography, to see what it's made of, seeing as there's no DNA to speak of. Do you have anyone who's good at mapping? I'd like to plot where the samples were found. Not to mention the current alien population is sourced from only one set of samples. There might be different species on the other samples we haven't even considered yet…"

The doughnuts arrived and were demolished by the time they'd finished the prioritised list, and it was another hour before they'd turned it into a coherent plan.

"And that's just this week. I've been told to prepare to move to bigger, better facilities as soon as Vasse can source them, plus hire more staff," Aliana said. "I'll send you any and all results as we get them, so you can start thinking about what else you'd like us to do."

Pandora could scarcely breathe. Only yesterday, she'd been doing everything herself after hours, and now she had a veritable army of qualified lab techs working under her. It was a little like dying and going to heaven, except without having to die first.

And she had a date with Prometheus to look forward to! Life couldn't get better than this.

FIFTEEN

Pandora only owned one special occasion dress — one she'd taken everywhere since leaving Earth — so getting ready for her date took surprisingly little time. Maybe not getting any biscuits had been good for her, because it fitted just as well as it had at her PhD graduation ceremony on Mars.

What if Prometheus didn't like it? It was fairly conservative, after all, with a puffy, knee-length skirt, a high collar and little cap sleeves, despite being called a pin-up dress. She even had an old-fashioned petticoat to go with it, though she didn't have it on now. There was such a thing as too much puff in the skirt.

Pandora pinned her hair back from her face, then changed her mind and settled on a messy French twist instead, clipped at the top with a bow that matched the pattern on her dress.

She finished the outfit with her only pair of heels, which she'd had custom made on Mars. Custom 3D printed, actually, but they'd been a graduation treat she was glad she'd allowed herself.

Pandora took a long look in her apartment's only mirror. Stars, she looked like an ancient housewife! She had to change. But into what?

Too late. The doorbell chimed. Prometheus was precisely on time.

Pandora swallowed. Before she could lose her courage, she palmed open the door.

Prometheus's eyes widened as his jaw dropped. "Oh, wow."

Her courage died. "I'll go find something

else to wear."

"No, please. It's perfect. Like an atomic age pinup come to life. You are, I mean. Stars, I'm not usually this tongue-tied. My only excuse is that I've only seen your face until today. To see you like this…I'm worried I'm underdressed." He gestured at his clothes, inviting Pandora to look her fill.

His well-tailored shirt shimmered like real silk, emphasising his broad shoulders and tapering to his waist. Of course, his dress pants fitted perfectly in front…though the real test was whether they clung to his backside right, not that she was going to say that. And, stars take it, it wasn't fair that he smelled even better than he looked. Like a forest after rain, with just a hint of earthiness.

"Do I look good enough to be seen with you?"

She nodded, not trusting her tongue to say anything that wouldn't embarrass her.

"We're close enough to walk to the restaurant if you like, or we could take a skimmer?"

Her mouth went dry. Riding a two-person skimmer, pressed against him, wasn't the best idea. "I'd like to walk," she found herself saying.

Prometheus held out his arm, for all the world like some old-fashioned denizen of the atomic age. "Shall we?"

Stars take it. She tucked her arm through his and they set off.

SIXTEEN

Prometheus had never believed in love at first sight. He'd known Nihal for years until that one disastrous night when he'd known they'd never be more than friends, if he hadn't ruined that.

But when Pandora tucked her arm through his, it was like Ghost had felled him with a bolt of lightning. From the moment he'd seen her, he'd been dying to ask her if she was wearing a petticoat under that skirt, but he hadn't dared.

He knew there were rules about first dates, and asking a girl about her underwear, or telling her about his most cherished sexual fantasy were definitely not on the list of acceptable conversation topics.

If only this were a real date, and not a prelude to what might be a very challenging interview.

He sighed. "I have a confession to make, and I owe you an apology."

"Mmm?"

He took this as his invitation to continue. "When I asked you on a date, that's all I had in mind, but my boss has me working tonight. All I can manage is a quick dinner, and then I have to go back to the studio to interview the CEO of Vasse Prospecting about what your alien discovery means for their mining plans for Gamma. My boss wants me to bring you, so you can provide balance to the debate, but I refuse to do that to you. It's poor thanks for the amazing interview you've already done."

She stopped and looked up at him, her eyes

thoughtful. "I knew there had to be more to it. My work colleagues were right. Someone like you wouldn't ask someone like me out on a date without a good reason for it." Her arm slid from his and she turned to go.

"No, please! I promised you dinner, and I am a man of my word. I've booked a table for two at Forge, and while I admit I talked the network into paying for it, I swear it's where I would have taken you on a first date anyway. Their chef does magical things in the kitchen." Prometheus dropped to his knees, his hands clasped in supplication. "Please, just have dinner with me. Then I'll take you home, before I go to the studio. I'll tell them you weren't interested."

She shook her head. "I must be crazy, but...all right."

"You won't regret it, I promise. Like I said, their chef...magic, I swear." He didn't dare offer his arm again, but she kept pace beside him all the way to Forge.

He'd hoped to find Vulcan at the bar, but it

looked like it was Nihal's night. As Nihal's critical eye scrutinised Pandora, he begged her silently with his eyes not to mess this up for him. Arnold had done enough.

Nihal gave the tiniest nod, before turning on her best smile for Pandora. "Whatever you do, don't let him leave before you've had dessert. We had a delivery of fresh strawberries this afternoon." She signalled a waitress to take them to their table.

Prometheus barely tasted the food, and he couldn't have said what he drank. He only had eyes for Pandora.

They talked about pets, families, and all the other things they'd left behind on Earth and Alba, respectively. It turned out that journalism school on Alba had been just as ruled by politics as the xenobiology department at Mars University, which was how she'd ended up as the manager of a geology lab, instead of peering at more Martian microbes under a microscope.

She was every bit as captivating in person as

she'd been on the screen. More, especially in that stars-crossed dress that looked like it had leaped, fully formed, out of his fantasies.

If there was one thing Prometheus knew now, it was that he was hopelessly infatuated with Dr Pandora Box.

But time was running out – that Vasse interview crept inexorably closer. Reluctantly, he set down his napkin.

"Look, I have to go. The interview, like I said. But you can stay – order dessert, with those strawberries Nihal told you about. They already know to charge it to my credit chip." He'd give anything for another hour with her. Ha, he'd sell his soul to spend the whole night with her, even if all he learned was whether she wore a petticoat under that skirt.

Pandora rose to her feet, smoothing her skirt. "Actually, I'm allergic to strawberries. I haven't been using the antihistamine patches here because there haven't been any, but I suppose I'll have to start again."

"I'll take you home, then."

"Actually, I'd like to go to the studio with you. I don't want you to get in trouble with your boss, not if he asked you to bring me. But I give you fair warning – I get terrible stage fright. It's why I took a job as a lab manager instead of a lecturer after I got my PhD. The moment I get up in front of a crowd, I just freeze up and can't speak. You wait, I bet I go all clammy the moment I step into the studio. Then you can take me home."

Prometheus could barely believe his ears. "Seriously, you'd do that for me?"

She gave a slow nod, then smiled. "I really enjoyed dinner, and I admit I want to hear more about those hell bunnies you had as pets. How do you get hell bunnies, anyway?"

"Well, there's a joke on Alba, or there was, that there's nothing a demon won't have sex with, especially the ones that are part shifter, and one of them must have shifted into a rabbit and…"

"Oh, no, I'm sure bestiality is one of those things you're not supposed to discuss on a first date," Pandora said. Then she muttered something that sounded like, "But still not as bad as doing ass to mouth."

Prometheus's mouth seemed to have a mind of its own tonight. "Oh, I agree. I never go ass to mouth. Terribly unsanitary."

Pandora looked shocked for a moment, then burst out laughing. It was music to Prometheus's ears.

She linked her arm with his. "So what do you like?"

"You. In this dress. If I ask you out on another date, a real one this time, would you do me a huge favour and wear this dress again? With maybe even a…petticoat underneath?" Well, he'd already broken the rules twice now. Maybe the third time was the charm.

"Yes. If you ask me," she said.

"Ask you to wear a petticoat?"

"No, ask me out on another date."

"Will you go out with me again? Maybe dinner and a show? Say, Friday afternoon and evening, so we can see the show first, and have dinner after?"

"Yes."

Prometheus's feet felt like they were floating all the way to the studio.

SEVENTEEN

Every moment she spent in the studio, Pandora expected her stage fright to make an appearance, but everyone was so nice, only pausing to briefly touch up her hair and makeup, before settling her on a couch that could have been the twin to the one in her apartment. There was no audience, just her, Prometheus, a couple of cameramen hidden in the shadows, and a woman with so many nervous tics she could scarcely stand still, who

Prometheus told her was the production assistant.

Everyone fell silent when Stella Vasse entered the studio. Elegantly clad in a black suit that sparkled under the lights like she carried her own galaxy with her, she commanded every eye as she seated herself on an armchair that Pandora swore had transformed into a throne.

Pandora's mouth went dry. Oh, there was the stage fright.

Then Stella jerked her head, and stared at Pandora. Her small smile turned into something more beaming as she crossed the floor to offer her hand to Pandora.

"Dr Pandora Box! Finally we meet! I've been trying to come to the Colony to meet with you since it opened, and I can't believe it's taken me this long. Are the labs to your satisfaction?"

Confusion beat stage fright, hands down. "Well, it's not like Mars, but we manage."

Stella frowned. "You mean your new labs

aren't ready yet? I gave particular instructions that your team should have access to them immediately. Let me speak to my assistant." She tapped her bracelet, and a holographic tablet appeared in the air above her wrist. "Dani, what's the delay with the new xenobiology research labs?"

A sleepy voice issued from the bracelet. "It's the weekend, Ms Vasse. The ribbon cutting isn't until Monday."

"Oh." Stella ended the call. A faint flush coloured her cheeks. "Well, that was embarrassing. I don't usually travel without my assistant, but I thought I could manage one short interview…" She shook her head. "Dr Box, when you take possession of your new research centre on Monday, please contact me if there is anything else you need."

"Well, I'm sure the labs are fine, but if you want me to really study this new alien microbe, we'll need to know its extent, the habitats it prefers…in short, we'll need another extended expedition to Gamma." Not that they'd know enough about the alien species for at least a few years, but it would likely take that long to get an expedition up and running. Mapping the microbes on Mars had taken decades, and the researchers had only need light EV suits. For exploring Gamma, she didn't even know if the protective gear existed yet.

Stella simply nodded, as if she dealt with impossible problems every day. "Leave it with me." She returned to her throne. Armchair. Whatever it was. Pandora wasn't sure any more. Stella was like no one else Pandora had ever met. "Shall we start the interview now? I'm sure I'll have a meeting in the morning I won't want to sleep through."

Stella started out doing most of the talking, answering Prometheus's questions with the skill of someone who'd learned to deal with the media probably at the same time as she'd learned to read or balance a budget sheet. Then the questions turned to what Vasse was doing about the aliens on its new mining claim on Gamma. Stella just smiled and said, "We're funding a new research institute, headed by Dr Pandora Box, to learn as much as we can about our alien neighbours. We know so little about them, and Vasse Prospecting is committed to protecting the environment before, during and after extraction. We want to know how best to preserve our alien neighbours, so that maybe one day, they'll be our allies. How they'll fit into the Titan-Human alliance, I have no idea, but I'm excited to find out.

"But Dr Box here is the expert. Dr Box, tell us, have you learned the aliens' language yet, so we can both sign a peace treaty?"

Pandora laughed. "I don't think the microbes are sentient, or intelligent enough to have a language of their own. Perhaps they might evolve into a sentient species, if left alone long enough, but it won't be in my lifetime. Here's what we do know about them…"

She described their unusual cell structure, if the individual units could indeed be called cells, and the crystalline structure that took the place of DNA, or at least her team thought it did. She talked until Prometheus handed her a glass of water, which she emptied in record time, before she stared at the glass. "That's one thing we have in common. Water. We both need water to live. Without it, it's just dust. Lifeless dust."

For the first time, she sympathised with the alien microbe, whatever it was. She couldn't imagine being stuck in a sample tube, or even down on the surface of Gamma, waiting patiently for the smallest drop of water to wake her from a deathly sleep. It sounded like a fairytale.

She turned to Prometheus. "Can I ask you a question?"

He looked surprised, but said, "Sure."

"When you were on Gamma, and the alien microbe was on you, were you the only one?"

"I was," he said slowly.

"Was there any water where you were?"

"There was no water on the surface at all.

Plenty in the atmosphere, but not as a liquid, no. One of the guys spilled the contents of his canteen on me. When it hit the dust, it just sort of…grew."

Stella smiled. "So maybe we have a lot in common with our alien neighbours. Something to think about, as we learn more about them. I'm certainly looking forward to hearing more about what Dr Box finds."

The interview ended soon after that, and Stella insisted on taking Pandora home. Pandora didn't dare refuse.

It wasn't until she was home in bed, her dress already circulating through a wash cycle, that she dared to admit to herself that she wished Prometheus had walked her home. She'd probably only see him on her screen after this, now he'd gotten his interview.

EIGHTEEN

On Friday afternoon, as promised, Prometheus presented himself at the reception desk of Vasse Geology Laboratories. There was no one at the desk, but there was an old fashioned bell, which he plied vigorously until an annoyed older man appeared. "Yes, what is it?" the man snapped.

"I'm here to see Pandora," Prometheus said pleasantly.

The man's frown deepened. "Dora should

have answered the bell. Don't know where she is today. I'll page her. Want a coffee while you wait?"

When Prometheus nodded, the man led him into the maze of corridors behind the reception desk, until they emerged into a small break room. One that didn't look like it had been cleaned for at least a week.

The man then disappeared, so Prometheus presumed he was supposed to make his own coffee, but the selection of dirty cups and gritty teaspoons gave him the distinct impression that he'd be risking food poisoning or worse if he ate or drank anything here, so he settled down to wait.

He didn't have to wait long. A procession of men in lab coats entered the room. They evidently had more resilient constitutions than Prometheus, for they soon occupied all the available seats, sipping coffee like their lives depended on it.

Then one of them sniggered. "How bad is Dora in bed? Does she really go ass to mouth?"

Prometheus wasn't sure who the question was directed at, though it looked like the man had asked his murky coffee, which kept its secrets close, if indeed it had any.

He decided to ignore the man and his questions. The others seemed to agree.

"What's a man need to do to get his research on the news?" This was definitely addressed to Prometheus. "I've stumbled across the biggest rhodium deposit you've ever seen."

"I bet you get lots of chicks, being on the news and all. How many have you fucked this week?"

"I found a whole asteroid made of gold once. All shiny, just like a star. I figured if I towed it home, I'd be the richest man in the whole system. Just gotta earn enough credits to get my own ship, so I can go out and get it. They must pay you a lot to be on TV and all. Will you give me enough credits?"

"When you go ass to mouth, do you make

her drink it all? Because you gotta blow in her mouth..."

The door opened, and Pandora breezed in, a vision in that beautiful dress. "I'm so sorry. I don't work here any more. Stella really did open a new research institute on the other side of the square, and I work there now."

"Good. Because your old colleagues here are complete dicks," Prometheus said, rising.

Pandora looked like she was trying hard not to laugh. "Shall we go?"

"Stars, yes."

NINETEEN

When the skimmer slowed to a halt, Pandora found herself outside a building she'd never entered before. "The Lovers' Arms. Um, forgive me if I'm wrong, but this looks like..."

Prometheus grinned. "The name you're looking for is love hotel. On the ground level, they have the most amazing cabaret lounge, with shows every night, and on the other levels – upstairs and down, seeing as some things are best done in the basement – are all full of themed rooms, which can be hired by the hour."

"And you've used these rooms?" Pandora asked, not sure she wanted to know the answer.

That grin didn't fade. "Actually, no. But the day before they opened, I did get to tour the place with a film crew, for a feature on new business ventures in the Colony."

"Oh. So you haven't…?"

"While some of the rooms are quite intriguing, I haven't met anyone I'd like to share them with for an hour, much less a whole night." He raised his eyebrows. "Unless you'd like a tour. The dominatrix dungeons come in a selection of colours, with matching whips, if you're still angry with me about dragging you to an interview when we were supposed to be on a date. I would only be too happy to submit to your punishment, if that means you'll forgive me."

She shook her head. "You know, I'm not sure whether you're joking or serious."

"Me neither."

That made her laugh. "Truly, I'm not mad at you for last week. My work colleagues had me convinced you could never really want to date me, and I never believed you'd actually turn up tonight, or I would have told you to meet me at the new lab instead of the old one."

"Your colleagues are dicks. Men I sincerely hope have to pay for sex for the remainder of their lives, thus safely eradicating their brand of misogyny from the gene pool. If I hadn't met them, I wouldn't have believed those kind of men could actually survive on Earth."

"They probably wouldn't have. But in an exploration vessel, with just them, on the edge of the Solar System for months or sometimes even years at a time, sometimes the crews just get a bit…strange. Or maybe it's just that strange people are attracted to that life. I don't know. There are all-female crews, too. Stella told me she flew with one for a few months when she first joined her family's business. They even brought their kids aboard — talk about distance schooling!" She laughed, hoping he couldn't see how nervous she was. She'd never been inside a brothel before, and this was…a big step.

"Pandora, if I've made a mistake, tell me and I'll take you to Forge for dinner, I swear. I didn't bring you here to seduce you, though I won't deny I'm willing if you are. Wait…forget I said that. Please." He ran a hand through his hair. "Stars, I feel like a teenager again when I'm around you. Scared to open my mouth, because I know the wrong words will come out. Okay. I…I brought you here because the cabaret bar really is amazing. The dancers are truly talented, even if the costumes are…well, a bit skimpy. They've been running an underwater show for a while now, but in honour of your discovery, they've been working on a new one, which they're calling First Contact. Lots of fire and light, with some djinn and a bunch of demons and other Titans with fire affinities. They invited me to come see a dress rehearsal, before the show goes live to the public. I asked if I could bring you, and they said yes. The kitchen's open just for us, and the chef has promised to cook us up a seafood feast better than anything you've ever eaten on Earth."

"I couldn't afford seafood on Earth," Pandora admitted. "I think I had a prawn cocktail at a wedding once. It was a cup full of lettuce and tomato and sauce, with half a tiny shrimp on top. I never knew if it was a real shrimp, or something made out of fish and shaped to look like one."

"Then tonight, I'll ask them to make you a real prawn cocktail. Along with…well, I know some of the water cabaret performers are Mer, so they get a discount at the aquaculture farm. There'll be more seafood than you can eat, I promise."

She couldn't believe what she was thinking, but she had to be certain. "Let me get this straight. You've brought me here so that I can see a private show before anyone else in the Colony, and afterward there will be an amazing dinner. But if I want, you'll take me to Forge instead?"

"Or anywhere else you want. Anywhere in the Colony."

Pandora closed her eyes. "I'm beginning to think you're mad."

"Or that you're mad to be on a date with me?"

"Oh, I know I'm crazy. I just…keep expecting to wake up and find that all this – with you, the alien microbe, and all the changes at work – will be nothing but a lovely dream."

"Will it still be a lovely dream if you go inside a love hotel to watch a brand new cabaret show?" he asked.

Pandora wet her lips. "I won't know until I see it, will I?"

"Are we going in?" He held out his arm.

She took it. "Indeed we are." And together, they stepped through the doors.

TWENTY

Melete had given them the best table, as usual – front and centre, with the best view of the stage, which sat atop the water tank. Likely a precaution in case the fire got out of control.

Pandora still seemed nervous, but Prometheus couldn't help but admire her courage. She'd worn the dress again, now adorned with an extra lace border along the hem, which likely belonged to the promised petticoat. Stars, but she was a living, breathing fantasy just sitting beside him.

The show began, taking him by surprise as all the lights went out. Then glowing red and orange spotlights hit the stage, and the silhouette of a heavily muscled man. Prometheus knew it was meant to represent him in his stone golem form, standing on the surface of Gamma, as the lights began to ripple, wraithlike shapes peeling away from the silhouette to caress him. It. The shadowed man, or whatever he was.

Before his eyes, the stage became a massive, fiery orgy, as what looked like at least a dozen dancers circled around the stoic standing figure. Prometheus shifted in his seat. This was getting mighty uncomfortable.

And then the colossus moved, swaying with the other dancers, dancing with each in turn, until he found his true match, a woman with curves that seemed to flicker like flames. Then she alone wrapped him round, until Prometheus wasn't sure whether she had limbs or tentacles, or it was all a trick of the light, and she engulfed him, moving with him in a more intimate dance than before.

Stars, if the alien had done that to him on Gamma...

Beside him, Pandora let out a moan.

"Are you all right?" he asked, his attention instantly on her.

"No. I want...I need..." She seized his hand, guiding him through the layers of lace and tulle to the hot, wet heat of her. "Please."

Caught in the same seductive spell, he couldn't do anything but obey, pressing his thumb exactly where she wanted it, while slipping a finger inside her. Circling, ever circling, to give her the blessed release she ached for.

Pandora's lips parted, her head thrown back, as she tightened around his finger. Close, so close...

She let out a small, strangled cry, barely audible as the music reached its crescendo, before the performance ended and darkness descended again.

When the lights came back on, they sat demurely apart, her skirt as smooth as if nothing had happened. Only the flush of her cheeks gave away what he'd done.

The performers lined up on the stage and took their bows as Pandora and Prometheus clapped. Prometheus could have sworn the colossus – an incubus, he was sure of it – winked at him, before taking another bow.

The flaming djinn woman the incubus had chosen as his paramour stepped into the middle of the stage, as the rest of the cast headed for their dressing rooms. "If you'd like a private room, we have a whole floor of themed rooms, devoted to the delights of flame." She stared directly at Pandora as she said it.

Pandora rose to her feet. "No. It was a lovely show, very stirring, but I think I'd like to go now."

Prometheus rose to his feet, resignation slowing his movements. He'd stuffed up again, he was sure of it. "Would you like me to take you home? Or just somewhere else for dinner?"

"Home would be great," she said, not even looking at him as she marched out of the bar.

It wasn't until they reached the street outside that she stopped. "Where do you live, anyway?"

Hardly daring to hope, he said, "I have an apartment in the Arena Dome, overlooking the Arena. Occasionally, if I'm home, I can catch a glimpse of the dragon battles from the balcony."

"Do you have a big bed?"

Big and sturdy, in case he accidentally turned into his golem form in his sleep. Not that he did that often, but it only took one time to break the bed, as he'd learned in the past. Back on Alba, he'd slept on a mattress on the floor.

"Yes."

"Let's go there, then."

Prometheus wanted nothing more than to do what she asked, but he was too stars-crossed chivalrous for his own good. "You don't really want this. You're under the spell of an incubus, the one onstage at the club. Even I felt it, and that spell doesn't usually work on a golem like me, so it had to be a pretty strong one. Or maybe because there were just the two of us, it was concentrated on us. I don't know. The thing is, it isn't you talking. It's the spell. You don't really want to…"

"Oh, yes I do. Do you know how many times I wanted to turn around and wrap my legs around your waist on the skimmer ride here?"

No.

"Or how I almost told Stella, the boss of my whole company, that I didn't want her to give me a lift home, because I wanted to invite you up to my apartment that night instead?"

"I don't deserve you," he said.

"I…I don't know what to think any more."

Prometheus sighed. More than anything, he wanted Pandora, but she had to know the truth first. How the whole April Fool's Day joke had started.

"Tell you what. Let's take an aircar to my place, maybe have some dinner, and then…see what happens." And while they ate, he could tell her. He owed her that much.

"Deal."

TWENTY ONE

They had the aircar to themselves, despite it still being daylight outside. Maybe she really was crazy, or maybe it was the incubus's spell that had suddenly made things clear, but she wasn't going to let this chance pass her by.

When Prometheus sat down, she climbed into his lap, facing him. Her skirt spread like a pool around them, hiding both her desire and his.

She took a deep breath. She'd never done

something this brazen before. "I want to feel more than your fingers inside me. Give me a proper release, Prometheus."

In her head, her colleagues laughed at her, telling her there was no way he could possibly want her.

But the erection straining to escape from his pants told her a different, far more primal tale.

She wasn't sure who unfastened his pants, her or him, but the moment she felt the heat of him inside her, she no longer cared. She rode him hard and fast, so intent on her own pleasure she paid scant attention to his, until she reached the cusp of her orgasm, and paused for the smallest instant to savour the anticipation until she hurtled over that cliff, his roar drowning out any sound she made.

Panting, she slumped against his chest. Stars, he was still inside her. She'd felt his release. How was he still hard?

She must have said it aloud, because she heard his hoarse voice in her ear: "I'm a golem. Living stone. Half earth elemental, half fire elemental. I can be made of stone, solid or molten, or flesh that's just a little harder than a normal human. I can do a partial shift, too, so parts of me are harder or hotter. Whatever you like."

She rocked her hips, so he rubbed against the right spot, then again. "I like."

"Wait, Pandora. There's something you need to know. About...the news story. That first interview."

"When I finished the interview with you, my underwear was soaked. You did that just with your voice," she admitted.

"Stars, that's...that makes it even harder to say this."

She started rocking again. He was going to tell her he wasn't interested in her, that this meant nothing to him, that...

"It was a joke. It was meant to be a joke. We doctored the footage from the Gamma expedition, so the dust glowed, and looked like it was alien life. I'd originally intended to let the joke run its course over April Fool's Day, and not tell anyone it was a hoax until the next day. Even when your call came through, I thought it was part of the joke, something one of the other guys had cooked up. But then I started talking to you, and I realised…it wasn't a joke, it was your job, and I'd made a joke out of it, and I didn't have the heart to tell you, or know how to apologise…"

Another orgasm ripped through her, so she didn't hear what he said next, until the pleasure faded.

"So I'm no better than the dicks you work with, or used to work with," Prometheus finished.

She'd take his dick any time of the day or night, she thought muzzily. He was nothing like the others.

She wet her lips. "You're not. You're nothing like them. I know I should be angry, that you turned aliens into a joke, but…I'm not. You never once made me feel like my job, my research was a joke. You always took me seriously, from the very beginning. I mean, are you going to tell anyone that it was a joke now?"

Prometheus shook his head. "Because it isn't. Not now."

"I should be thanking you. Your joke turned into the most amazing opportunity, turning my life around and upside down and making things I hadn't believed possible come true. Even us." She thought for a moment. Stars, it was so distracting sitting in his lap. But she had to concentrate. Something about the video. That first video… "I always knew there was something wrong with the footage. That it was fake. It's the glow. It only glows when Gamma's in night, or the lights are off in the lab. In daytime, even with Gamma's overcast skies, it doesn't glow. You faked the glow, didn't you? That's the only way it makes sense…"

He nodded. "Can you ever forgive me?"

"That depends."

"On what?"

"Whether you want to take me back to your

place. If you want another date. Whether we get arrested for having sex in a public aircar."

"Yes and yes and I hope not, because I'm not sure I'd forgive myself if I was responsible for you getting arrested."

She had to smile. "That's actually kind of sweet." Her tablet chimed with an incoming message. She wanted to ignore it, but it was Friday afternoon – still the work day for everyone else, even if she'd taken an afternoon off. She slid out of Prometheus's lap and onto the seat beside him to read the message. "It's from Stella. She says the *Truella* has been refitted with a complete xenobiology suite, and it's at my disposal as of Monday. She says she has a Titan crew who can survive on the surface and take any samples I want, while I stay aboard the ship in orbit to direct the expedition. She wants me to hire a dedicated media manager, though, to document the expedition. She wants maximum press coverage for this."

Prometheus raised his hand. "I volunteer."

"You want to go back to Gamma?"

He grinned. "Actually, no, I don't care much about Gamma at all, but the illegal aircar sex we just had was amazing, better than my most elaborate fantasies, and I want to go wherever you do. So, sign me up."

She smiled back. "Ask me again on Monday. After we've spent all weekend together."

"I won't change my mind," he promised, leading the way out of the aircar.

"Yeah, but…that's work. And right now, it's the weekend, and our first date. We've broken a whole bundle of first date rules, which makes me wonder if we can break them all by Monday. I mean, the no sex on a first date rule was just begging to be broken. Pounded into oblivion by…"

"Me. Definitely me."

They arrived at Prometheus's apartment then, and it took only a moment for him to palm open the door before he carried her to the bed. The enormous, solid, nigh on unbreakable bed.

"Is there a rule about breaking beds on the first date?"

"I don't know, but if you want, we can give it a try."

"I think I love you."

"I think I love you, too."

TWENTY TWO

"Are you sure someone lives here?" Pandora asked, eyeing off the trees in the Arbor Dome.

"Of course. Ghost had this house built specially."

"Is it a tree house?"

"No, it's a normal house. Well, it's big and more luxurious than most places in the Colony, but he swears he found the plans for it in the archives somewhere, and modified it so it's more comfortable, better for a family."

"He has kids?"

"Just one. His fiancée, Maia, is a midwife. She'll be here, too."

"Was she in on the joke as well?"

"No, only me, Vulcan, Achilles and Ghost knew about it. They didn't even know what the joke was, just that I needed the video from the Gamma expedition."

"Have you told them the truth now?"

Prometheus hesitated. "I may have mentioned there'd been a change of plans at our last poker night. I did thank them for their help, though. Bought them a round of drinks."

So the joke that wasn't a joke wouldn't be an issue. She still felt nervous, though. Maybe because she was meeting so many people.

"There's the house!"

Pandora blinked in surprise. The trees just sort of thinned, and in the clearing stood a lovely log cabin, the sort that she'd only seen on pictures of luxury tourist ranches. "This is amazing!"

Nihal and a man Pandora didn't know

appeared from between the trees. "Wait until you see the chickens," he said, pointing.

"They're green!" she exclaimed.

The man looked proud. "Chimeras. Part chicken, part lettuce. I'm responsible for most of the chimeras in the Colony, though that'll change soon, when Nihal's brewery takes off."

"You must be Orel, the third and most mysterious partner in the business," Prometheus said. "Vulcan mentioned you, but he didn't say if he wanted you included in any of the media."

Orel shook his head. "I'm not someone who likes being in the public eye. I'm much better behind the scenes. Right, sweetness?" He kissed Nihal, which made her blush.

"We should probably go inside. Everyone else should have already arrived," Nihal said, leading the way.

Inside meant the backyard, where a whole crowd of people hung around a barbeque and some tables of food.

A small woman caught sight of them and

clapped her hands. "Right, now we're all here…time for introductions!"

She pointed at a man in a cowboy hat, and the silvery woman standing beside him. "For anyone who doesn't know, this is Rana and Byron. He runs a ranch under the Arena Dome, and he has access to a secret banana supply. She works for the Watch, so watch yourselves if you're thinking of stealing any of my chicken salads!"

She sidled up to the bloke at the barbeque and slapped his backside. "I'm Maia, and this is Ghost, search and rescue specialist, who has saved more lives than anyone I know, including mine and our son, Christos. Who is currently having his nap so we can enjoy a bit of adult conversation before I have to open the milk bar again."

"Over on the veranda, that's Vulcan and Hestia. She's the Colony librarian, so if there's a book you want, or you need something new to read, she's the one to ask. Vulcan, as I'm sure you all know, is the owner of Forge and possibly the most brilliant dancer in the Altan System."

Vulcan opened his mouth to protest, but Hestia hushed him.

"Orel is one of the bioengineers at Eden Labs, creator of the lovely chimeras that provided ingredients for the salads on the table today, and soon to be business partner of Nihal and Vulcan in Forge's new brewery. Nihal, of course, is the head brewer, and you have her to thank for the drinks today.

"Over in the corner, by the chickens, is Achilles, the Battle Master of the Arena. Despite my strong suggestion, he didn't bring a date, because he's a confirmed bachelor. Or so he thinks!"

Laughter erupted from all the couples. In fact, it looked like he was the only single there. How strange.

"Helping Ghost out on the barbeque by keeping him company are Valentine and Anna. They were actually married before leaving the Solar System, but were separated when the

Magellan was shot down during the war. After a salvage crew found his badly damaged escape pod, the regeneration team at the Colony hospital helped put him back together again, so he could join Anna here in the Colony.

"Now, last are a couple we all know from the recent news, and they need no introduction. Prometheus and Pandora, welcome to our new house."

Maia grabbed a drink, then lifted it into the air. "We've been in this house for a little while now, but it's not truly a home until it's had a housewarming, celebrated with lots of good food and good friends. I know we've come from all over the galaxy, Humans and Titans, on both sides of a hard fought war, but we're here in the Colony, together, now, and this is our home. You all are always welcome here, and may there always be more that brings us together than drives us apart. And if anyone's thinking of causing trouble…" She raised a fist in the air. "Stars help them, because no one's going to take our Colony from us!"

Cheers erupted, before everyone drank to her toast. It was a strange one, and a strange bunch of people, but somehow, Pandora felt it was right. If so many people could come together to find a sort of family together here, across all that separated them, then maybe there was hope for the galaxy.

ABOUT THE AUTHOR

Demelza Carlton has always loved the ocean, but on her first snorkelling trip she found she was afraid of fish.

She has since swum with sea lions, sharks and sea cucumbers and stood on spray drenched cliffs over a seething sea as a seven-metre cyclonic swell surged in, shattering a shipwreck below.

Demelza now lives in Perth, Western Australia, the shark attack capital of the world.

The *Ocean's Gift* series was her first foray into fiction, followed by her suspense thriller *Nightmares* trilogy. She swears the *Mel Goes to Hell* series ambushed her on a crowded train and wouldn't leave her alone.

Want to know more? You can follow Demelza on Facebook, Twitter, YouTube or her website, Demelza Carlton's Place at:

www.demelzacarlton.com

More Books by Demelza Carlton

<u>Colony: Holiday series</u>

Cowboys and Aliens (#1)

Ghost (#2)

Vulcan (#3)

Cupid (#4)

Valentine(#5)

Prometheus (#6)

<u>**Colony: Aqua series**</u>

Halcyon (#1)

Poseidon (#2)

Apollo (#3)

<u>**Siren of Secrets series**</u>

Ocean's Secret (#1)

Ocean's Gift (#2)

Ocean's Infiltrator (#3)

<u>**Siren of War series**</u>

Ocean's Justice (#1)

Ocean's Widow (#2)

Ocean's Bride (#3)

Ocean's Rise (#4)

Ocean's War (#5)

How To Catch Crabs

<u>**Nightmares Trilogy**</u>

Nightmares of Caitlin Lockyer (#1)

Necessary Evil of Nathan Miller (#2)

Afterlife of Alana Miller (#3)

Romance a Medieval Fairytale series

Enchant: Beauty and the Beast Retold

Dance: Cinderella Retold

Fly: Goose Girl Retold

Revel: Twelve Dancing Princesses Retold

Silence: Little Mermaid Retold

Awaken: Sleeping Beauty Retold

Embellish: Brave Little Tailor Retold

Appease: Princess and the Pea Retold

Blow: Three Little Pigs Retold

Return: Hansel and Gretel Retold

Wish: Aladdin Retold

Melt: Snow Queen Retold

Spin: Rumpelstiltskin Retold

Kiss: Frog Prince Retold

Reflect: Snow White Retold

Roar: Goldilocks Retold

Cobble: Elves and the Shoemaker Retold

Float: Enchanted Horse Retold

Steal: Forty Thieves Retold

Call: Pied Piper Retold

Fall: Scheherazade Retold

Feather: Swan Maidens Retold

Cross: Billy Goats Gruff Retold

Weave: Rapunzel Retold

Claim: Puss in Boots Retold

Curse: Rose Red Retold

www.ingramcontent.com/pod-product-compliance
Lightning Source LLC
Chambersburg PA
CBHW071014180726
48291CB00004B/1451